A POET
from the Plains

by Patricia Ann Lynch

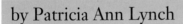

Strategy Focus

As you read, **monitor** your understanding of the poet's work. Reread to **clarify** anything that is unclear.

 HOUGHTON MIFFLIN   BOSTON

Key Vocabulary

beats the syllables in a line of poetry that sound strongest

imagery interesting words and descriptions that you can picture in your mind

lines rows of words in a poem

repetition a repeating pattern of sounds or words

rhyme a word that has the same last sound as another

rhythm a pattern of beats in poetry

sense words words that appeal to the five senses: sight, sound, smell, taste, and touch

stanzas groups of lines of poetry

Word Teaser

These are "poetry paragraphs."
What are they?

Virginia Driving Hawk Sneve (SNAY-vee) loves to write. She has written more than 20 books and many short stories. She also writes poems. She mostly writes about Native American life.

South Dakota

Rosebud Reservation

Virginia Driving Hawk Sneve is part of the Lakota Sioux tribe. She grew up on the Rosebud Reservation in South Dakota.

Virginia had a happy childhood. She loved to read. Once she came across a set of books called *The Book of Knowledge*. There were 20 books in the set. They were all very long. She read all 20 books twice!

Times were often hard for Virginia's family. There were not many jobs on the Rosebud Reservation. Sometimes her parents had to leave to find work. When Virginia's parents were away, her two grandmothers took care of her.

Virginia's grandmothers told her many tales. She loved to listen to them. She loved to learn about the history of the Lakota Sioux people. Later, she used what she learned to write many of her books.

Virginia Driving Hawk Sneve uses imagery in many of her poems. For example, she might describe a deep blue sky above a rose-colored mountain.

She also uses words that help readers think about sights, sounds, flavors, and feelings. She might describe a melting ice cream cone dripping over your hand. These are called sense words.

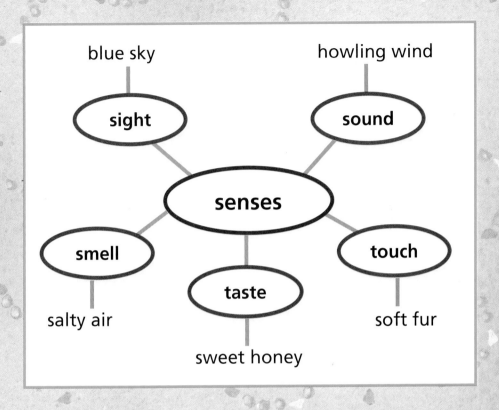

Some of Sneve's poems use repetition. Repeated sounds, words, and lines make her poems sound like music. Sometimes they use rhyme, too. How can you tell? In rhyme, the lines of words end with the same sounds. For example, *know*, *blow*, and *go* are words that rhyme.

One of Sneve's poems is called "I Watched an Eagle Soar." This poem has a special rhythm, or pattern of beats. All the lines in this short poem are grouped together. Groups of lines are called stanzas.

In 2000, Virginia Driving Hawk Sneve was given the National Humanities Medal. Sneve won it for sharing her wisdom about Native American culture.

Virginia Driving Hawk Sneve helps readers understand Native American life. She tells readers about Native Americans' proud past. She also tells about their hopeful future.